Dorrie stood over the freshly ma[de grave,] the gentle breeze that surrounde[d her] that morning drifted shyly past, ta[king the laughter and] the spirit of a young girl away with its gentle stroke.
The small framed woman stood, holding down the short shallow breaths of upset, condensing them from rising up in her chest and throat. She held them down, compressing them until a private moment alone where her sobs could be released.
She had married and buried her husband in a short space of time, but although she walked away knowing she would never see Herbert again she knew that there was no use in brutally testing love, bending its back into breaking and trying to bring on before time the grief she imagined was inevitable.
Dorrie stood watching the invisible ghosts of feelings that she freed into the air, she realised that moment love was the simple energy by which one is bound to the earth. Dorrie promised herself that the setting point of her emotions would be hope. Lying upon her heart.
 Hope would be her motivation for living, even when deep down she was empty, as the substance of love that once occupied her heart had now been harshly replaced with a huge lead weight of loneliness. She knew that the outcome of death would be devastating, if death won it would never let her believe in hope, it would wear down any belief she had ever had in anything until she died too, not physically but emotionally and mentally.

She did not want to switch off and let everything pass her by. All she had to live for were her four small children, if not, she pondered, would she return to an empty house laying abandoned slippers in front of the fire waiting for the key to turn in the door once more.
Dorrie buried her heart the same day she buried her husband. That day she watched it being lowered into the earth until she could no longer retrieve it.

Chapter 2

In 1946, the summer was a long and hot one; it was July of that year that Dorrie and Herbert were married. It was a humble ceremony in the Town Hall in Barnsley and a small party afterwards back at the family home, the fact that it was a small wedding didn't bother them in the slightest they just wanted to be man and wife. They had the blessing of Herberts family and Dorrie had settled quite easily into their fold.
Nellie and her husband Joseph were their witnesses; they were Herbert's sister and brother in law. Dorries

family did not attend. Her father longed too but his wishes were suppressed by her mother who disagreed with her daughter marrying the Yorkshire man. She thought he wasn't good enough for her daughter but then again always criticised any choice or plans that Dorrie had made for her.

Dorrie knew that when she packed her bag and headed off to Barnsley in search of Herbert that she quite frankly no longer cared for her mothers opinion on anything anymore. She didn't need her approval and wanted to make her own way in the world.

All her life Dorrie had tried to either pander to her mothers egotistical nature and also at the same time listen to her fathers heartache at the thought of his only daughter being driven away. They had a great relationship and she knew she could always count on his support throughout her life. She knew he didn't judge or comment much but just remained in her corner most of the time. Dorrie could no longer stand the daily battle she had at home and that contributed to her pursuit of Herbert. She thanked God it did too everyday, maybe the battlefield that she called home was the push in the right direction she needed, it forced her into a corner of which she emerged guard up and ready for the battle ahead. Dorrie knew that everything would work out in the end, even though she had to venture through an emotional storm with her family first to ensure it . She adored her father and knew he admired her strong spirit, to live for

the moment and make every minute count rather than being held back all the time by what if's.
Dorrie watched her parents life unfold and learnt through their mistakes. She knew she didn't want to succumb to a marriage of convenience and just fall into a mundane routine that would just take over her own existence as a person. Although her mother tried convincing her that her head was full of nonsense and she had to get to grip with the reality of every day married life she knew that her and Herbert would be different. She knew that her marriage would go the distance even to her mothers pleading that it wouldn't and that he was no good for her. Dorrie had felt an absence for so long and she realised that Herbert was what it was, she knew that she couldn't spend another minute of her life without him in it.
Even when she first met him she knew that it wouldn't be a case of a short lived romance she knew that more would evolve but she just had to seek it out to show him that she cared so deeply for him that they would never be apart again.

The day she arrived in Barnsley to find him his family were taken back by her gesture, it wasn't really something women do or should do for that matter. She didn't care for petty unwritten laws of society in this instance she just wanted to start living again and would have pulled out all the stops to do just this.
The small affair was a dream come true really for them both, the less fuss the better.

For sometime after, the newlyweds lived with Herbert's mother and father until they rented their first home together in Lea Road, Athersley. This did somewhat test their relationship as they were all together in a place Dorrie had not yet grown accustomed to this did not deter them however , it made them stronger.

With their first child already on the way also they made the most of their time when they were out of the house as they knew their short spell of time alone was drawing to an end.

They eagerly awaited the birth of their child and knew that this was only the beginning for them.

Herbert was going to make a great father , he was always kind and charming and had a great sense of humour. Dorrie could sit there in her chair back in London seeing the life she left behind playing out in her mind like an old Jimmy Stewart film. Those memories she kept, she didn't want to share them or dilute them as they would be retold and retold. She wanted to keep that part of her life with her so nobody could ever dispute the choices she made back then. She was proud that she had made them even though the outcome was not to be expected she knew that she followed her heart and sometimes that's all any of us can do.


It was only the previous year they were serving in the army, based in Belgium. It was there that they began their friendship and when the war had finally ended they had promised they would write and keep in touch, Dorrie left Herbert that last day not really sure if she would ever see him again and not knowing how he felt.

She went back to London to carry on with her life with no real insight into what the future held and feeling empty, she had known Herbert was originally from Barnsley but she had no geographical knowledge of the north.

This didn't stop them writing and keeping in touch, they knew that it was inevitable that if they didn't meet up or arrange something other than a few letters that time and distance would keep them apart forever.
The letters came regular and she read each one over and over until she could picture all the things Herbert spoke to her about and what he looked like and how Barnsley seemed so beautiful from what he described. The things that really stood out was the great sense of community it possessed even after some soldiers didn't come home, families were torn apart by the war and the way of life had almost over night taken a great pressure on its shoulders. This appealed to Dorrie, the fact that you could count on your community, not like London where it was sometimes you didn't even know your next door neighbours name, the fact that they ate their Yorkshire pudding as a starter for a roast dinner seemed odd to Dorrie but both odd and exciting. It seemed so laid back, no hustle and bustle to get on a bus or a train, no

coming home to sit in a room with the hostility of her mother oozing from the walls and no dictation of how her life should be or end up.

After a few more letters and a few months had passed Dorrie's memories ran dry from the small amount of time they shared ion Belgium so she packed her clothes and a few belongings and left her mother, father and brother behind to pursue the man she had met and start a knew life in Barnsley. She didn't tell Herbert she was coming she wanted to show how much she cared and knew that her actions spoke louder than any words they had ever exchanged over the months.

She was worried as she hadn't received a letter from him in a while and didn't want her mother to be right; that he had met someone else and gave up hope in Dorrie ever coming to visit.

Dorrie used all the time it took to travel to Barnsley to picture what his reaction would be when he saw her at his door, she pondered over the thought that she may have left it too long to go looking for him. When Dorrie arrived she went to Athersley to see if the correspondence address she had would still be where he was. She had promised herself as she left the train that if he wasn't here she would search a little, actually try to find him before she gave up and went back to London. Even though it was an idyllic future Dorrie prepared herself for the worst scenario still. If she had travelled there for nothing alone then at least she would know for certain how the story was destined to end.

She had no pictures of him only those created in her minds eye. When in Athersley she visited all the places that she thought may have been his frequents but was getting more disheartened as nothing was making her any the wiser. She knew he worked but she did not know which mine. She thought it was a small town where everyone would know him but it wasn't the case at all. Barnsley was a large town, larger than Edmonton and she was surprised how busy it was and how vibrant. She asked in a few small local shops and they couldn't help but she couldn't resist the bubbling feeling in the pit of her stomach that she was in fact getting closer to him.

She was approaching a local greengrocer when she felt the urge to try in there just to rule it out. A small plump lady at the counter answered her questions eagerly and informed her that Herbert's family lived in North Pavement. To Dorries delight she wasn't actually that far from there. After detailed directions from the elderly lady Dorrie ventured off to find what she had been waiting for, for so long in Barnsley.

Chapter 3

As the young slender stranger left the shop the keeper sighed, visioning what greatness lied ahead, as if awoke from a deep slumber she shook her head and smiled, quickly scurrying back off to what she had been doing. "That girl had a glint in her eye Harry, she was looking for Herbert Shaw". As usual, Harry was slumped in the chair fast asleep not knowing what his wife had just seen. She stood a while watching by the door watching the glow from the feelings that Dorrie had released into the air.

Dorrie passed houses upon houses whilst in search for Herbert, they all looked the same from the outside only differentiated by the colour of the doors; some red some blue.

North Pavement was not a particularly large street but to Dorrie it seemed never ending and her heart began to sink at each passing. The lady in the greengrocers never gave a number she began to wonder if she would seem desperate for knocking on a randomly picked door. What would she say? Before she could think again she found herself knocking the door of number 29.
Unusually a child answered the door then for a brief moment Dorrie realised she was not in London. It seemed like such a close community here, it was another world completely and Dorrie was drawn to be a part of it.

It was pure escapism, as if all the other towns in England had aged and changed but this one had not.

It was as surreal as a film, one where everything was perfect, and untouched. The little boy stood there patiently while Dorries thoughts were churning in her mind.

"Sorry I am looking for someone" Dorrie said conscious of her London accent. "Is your mother or father home?" Dorrie finished anxiously.

The boy said nothing and ran off down the hallway disappearing. A woman emerged from the doorway around Dorries age, she asked "Who you looking for lass?"

"A man named Herbert Shaw, you see I know him and, well we met in the war and I was told he lived around here" Dorrie rushed out, glad that the woman had not minded being fired a question.

"That'd be Doris she knows everybody!" replied the thick set woman. "They be at number 31, next door. Herbert lives in Sackville Street that next door is his sister Eleanor's house everyone calls her Nellie."

"Thank you so much, I have travelled from London to see him, sorry to have troubled you. I will go and try next door." Dorrie said wanting to run and beat the door down to see who was in.

"No trouble" The woman smiled again. They exchanged their goodbyes and Dorrie walked next door ready to see what she had felt like she had waited years for.

As she approached the door she felt a light dancing in her stomach somewhere deep down that she could no longer hold down, as she tapped the knocker, quietly mind, as she did not want to appear overly eager. The big blue door opened slowly as if there was going to be an outburst of surprise once fully opened. To Dorries' dismay there actually was. Herbert was standing there slowly looking up not believing his eyes.

"Don't just stand there love, drop your bags and come here" he boomed as if they had never been apart. Dorrie did as he asked and drew him close to her taking in every fibre of his being. He picked her up and span her around on the doorstep and Dorrie felt a flush of redness come over her face, she smiled shyly checking nobody was looking at them.

"Don't scare the poor lass away she has only just got here! Invite her in" came a gentle voice that belonged to Nellie, Herberts sister from over his shoulder Dorrie could see her standing there wiping her hands on her apron. Breaking the trance they had both gone into and straightening their clothes, Herbert picked up the small bags that Dorrie had travelled with he started to usher Dorrie towards the back of the house where the essence of fresh bread and strong tea was seeping. "I've just made a fresh pot, be nice to warm your belly. There is freshness in the air up her not like in London where Herbert said you are from". Nellie offered as she took Dorrie's coat and hat in two seconds flat.

They all assembled around a small wooden table. Dorrie and Herbert kept interrupting each other excitedly whilst Nellie ticked over in her head what cups and saucers to use for their lovely guest from the South.
The small framed woman came over to the table beaming, wanting to know everything about their soon to be lodger, of course her and Joe would put Dorrie up, that was if she was planning on staying long. Secretly Nellie hoped she was planning on staying, of all the silly young girls that had been hanging around Nellie knew this one was here to stay. Nellie knew she would come knocking all other contenders down with her bestowed grace.
Nellie watched as they eagerly caught up and watched how Herbert gently touched Dorries' arm each time she spoke. She studied the woman's face like a place of interest, remembering the long stories of her; the woman her brother had fallen in love with. Nellie placed the description Herbert had given her like a jig saw as she watched their movements; Nellie was in awe of her like everyone else was when this fine lady was in their presence

Dorrie was shown to a small room with a bed and a cabinet and a small wardrobe for her things. "Thank you for letting me stay Nellie, I do appreciate it I know I should have wrote and said that I was planning on visiting but I didn't really have time I just decided that I would come and that was that"

"Eh? Oh its no trouble really Dorrie, I knew that you would come one day, and there was no way Herbert would come to London. No offence like but here is just something else. I know that you will maybe find it hard at first but you will fit in just fine.It is a different way of life here, laid back and everyone knows everyone within a mile radius of their street, they will all be wondering who you are and what you are doing here. No doubt they will be baking anything going just to have an excuse to come in and have a nose."
Nellie said as she was making the bed up with fresh sheets. Dorrie was unpacking her things wondering what the rest of the day held in store for her and Herbert.

After Nellie had made the bed up Dorrie sat down and just sat there a minute and took a breath. She looked around her small room and thought that soon enough they should make a home for theirselves, she won't push though she will just wait for it to all happen naturally. She was just relieved that Herbert hadn't met someone else.

After about 10 minutes she walked along the hall to the bathroom and quickly freshened up with some cold water. She felt actually quite drained from the excitement and the journey and everything she was taking in along the way. Downstairs she heard Nellie talking to Herbert and it was in a muffled tone. She made herself known to be there in case it was anything private. She walked back into the kitchen and sat there waiting for the rest of the day to unfold.

Chapter 4

Once the years had passed Dorrie often thought to her self about what things might have been like if Herbert had lived. If science and pharmaceuticals were as advanced as they were now then his condition would have been detected, he could have been receiving treatment and his diabetes would have been under control. There were many a people who suffered because of the colliery work; it triggered different illnesses later in life. There wasn't much of a choice though back then apart from factories and perhaps shop work. Not like now where people have the patience to travel to high flying jobs and come home a long way all in the same day. Although now she had a comfortable life, she never wanted for anything, but she still felt that same emptiness she felt the day she lost Herbert. All the time that she often passed sitting in her chair wondering what would have been if he had lived to see his children grow up. She felt cheated and also felt a continuous grief of things that he had missed out on along the way not just with the children but other things like his opinion on matters in the house, what she needed from the shop and what she should wear when going to the school to see the teacher about David being a truant. All these memories she made were ones that she could just keep inside for her alone. She only had her children to share them with later on in life. She never really discussed her previous life though once she had met Doug. She just didn't feel it was apt really. The children must have had questions burning in the back of their throats, ones she should have answered but didn't know how to. There were times that she could have sat them round the table and told them more about their father and their short lived life in Barnsley but she couldn't, she felt once she lifted the lid on her feelings she would not be able to keep it shut once more. She feared this would open the floodgate for all the emotions she had buried a long long time ago. She knew that there were things that she should have shared but she often thought that she would speak of him no more and the pain would go away. She was often wrong and this pain came sometimes at night in her dreams, sometimes when she was just going about her daily routine and sometimes when she thought it wouldn't even enter her head at all.

Doug her new husband had the garden to tend to and to occupy his time and Dorrie threw all her time and energy into her family. Things were still tense with her mother, even after her father had died; she felt she could never build the bridges. Doug visited his mother in law and did odd jobs; he was more of a son to her than her own one. Dorries older brother was becoming a distant stranger although she saw her children, whom were all grown up and had lives of their own now; on a regular basis she had still been left to make a life for herself with Doug. She was proud that they had ambition and had amounted to something. They all seemed to have the drive that she possessed all those years ago as that alone was all that she had to cling to when she was left a widow with four small children those many years ago in Barnsley.

She adored her family and felt that same belonging burn in her throat when they came to see her. It brought tears to her eyes remembering what they had gone through when they were all so small.

The hardship they had survived and had thus strived to make sure they never knew poverty like it again. As a younger family they became a victim of circumstances, they lost their father and had no other family keeping them in Barnsley, Dorrie was promised a life again in London and a fresh start to rebuild herself again. Her mother had said that if she assisted the care of an elderly relative then she would be looked after in return.

In fact she was left to fend for herself and her family as well as caring full time for her invalid aunt who was bedridden. Dorrie kept trying to spin all her plates but in the end she dropped them all and had a breakdown.

For her own well being the children were taken into care and raised by a family until Dorrie had healed mentally. This was a hard battle and the first one Dorrie had to succumb to.

Dorrie still flitted back to these times and often wondered how she managed to have the strength to make it through the dark moments. She often felt a surge of euphoria to know that she had once again come out the other end of a tunnel that her mother had tried to corner her in.

In the summers since she had married Doug the garden was sprinkled with laughter when everyone was together again, Dorrie knew she was rich in the sense of being loved but poor in the sense of being in love. Something had remained in Barnsley that day was never replaced. Sometimes she couldn't wait to get to heaven again to fill that space.

Doug was her safety and comfort she knew things would stay consistent with him although to a stranger that may seem selfish; she and Doug were more like companions on the rest of their journey. "Enough of that " she shook her head gently and went out to the kitchen to put all the food back into the freezer that Jeff was getting out. She could hear him shouting "Chips" as she got out of her chair. Laughing to herself "oh I wouldn't change him for the world now."

Chapter 5

Once Dorrie and Herbert were married and had set up home their eldest son David came along and then at 18 month intervals came Pauline, Anthony and Susan.

Laughter and happiness coated their walls thickly and the young couple were very much in love and their time was occupied with their four small children.
Herbert was always making the children smile and laugh at his magic tricks and his larking about. Whatever came they managed to deal with and always made the most of their time as a family together. They would huddle together and stay in the warm when the winters hit and play games and just be together as a unit and when the summers came there was no keeping them in the house. They went for picnics, walks and adventures and filled up every minute of the days they spent.
The time used to fly by and the days rolled into one another. Dorrie had adjusted just fine to her knew way of life in Barnsley and had soon set into the laid back demeanour of others around her. She had soon forgotten about the busy town she had left behind and fell in love with her home and lifestyle.

Dorrie often smiled to herself about how wrong her mother had been those years ago when she had left London for Barnsley. She often missed her father though and the few friends she had made growing up. She wrote to her friends and her father as often as she could update them on the goings on in her new life. When they had the money they visited London which was seldom but the children liked it and they liked their grandfather and always asked when they would see him again. Herbert always kept the children entertained, they never had many luxuries but they were loved by all that surrounded them which compensated for any top of the range toy that was in the shop.

　Dorrie loved Herbert to the point of madness and she could never remember her life without him in it. Dorrie was never aware that their time together was limited. Do any of us really ever know when our journey has reached an end? Every now and again we are reminded of our own mortality and vow to make a little more effort with those we love as we never know really when our time has run out. We are all guilty of having the reoccurring feelings of "what if" and " I wish I had" but everything happens for a reason. The great coil of life as was Thomas Hardy's theory, that our actions and lives are destined in some way to make up this ever winding never-ending coil which ultimately proves that what we do can have a ripple effect with others, even though we may not realise it now sometimes it triggers later on in life when you are least expecting it.

　Grief makes us all selfish in one way or another; it makes us imprisoned briefly in lost moments with people who have passed away. It's a part of what makes us who we are as human beings without loss we do not know worth sometimes.

Time is a healer as the say but when something significant happens in our lives we all try to hold it together in fear that letting our guard down to expose feelings that we do not always want to share. When

Dorrie moved back to London after Herbert had passed away this is what she did. She tried to hold it together for her young family's sake. As they took Herbert out of the house on a stretcher she dreaded the words the doctor uttered to her days later. She didn't ever think that she would have to face life without him. When you are young and have no responsibilities it is common that love is seen as a disposable thing that is experimented with in a guiltless way. It becomes a quick fix to fill in the gaps that you know will be filled more permanently when you meet the "someone" who will accompany you on your journey through life. The life before you is seen in their eyes and when you capture that feeling you cant ever imagine your life without them in it, even the mere thought or contemplation of what it would be like is too distressing to face. You always fear the moment that you will have to face upto it the moment when they are gone and here you are alone to face the world once again, a part of you dies right along with them, it is partially retrievable if you have children as a part of them lives on Dorrie had her children to awaken her from the dark slumber that grief casts upon us all, she had fragments of Herbert around her for the rest of her life. Its easy to lose your way sometimes , wander off the path intended for you but the people who nudge you gently back on are the ones who count the ones that matter. Dorrie had her children to do that although she had lost her way and her soul mate she coped for a while. He mother sent for them to live in London again not too far from her and put them up in her

Aunts' house which seemed a great remedy when Dorrie was reading her letter. She was to live in the house and take care of her invalid aunt. Dorrie was going to get support from her mother and her family emotionally and the children would be able to start school. Dorrie thought this was the new start they needed and the children were excited about returning to London. They arrived and settled in again in no time and Dorrie went about her duties in the house but with no support from her family.

Dorrie was trapped with a mother who was never satisfied, an aunt who constantly needed attention and four children who had just lost their father. Torn between keeping everyone going and happy, Dorrie had a breakdown. The work with her aunt was too much and her mother had offered no help at all. Dorrie still did not lose hope she fought back and didn't succumb to the oblivion of never seeing her children again or returning to her aunt's house to cook and take care of her. Dorrie fought back and broke out the four corners of her mind to take control of her life once more and make sure that her children found all the comfort and support they needed in her alone. She got her children back out of the temporary care they had been placed in and made a life again in London in their own house away from any other responsibility and she promised herself she would make it work. She had to prove that life did carry on despite losing the core of her soul she would go on for her children's sake alone.

When Dorrie had first moved back to London from Barnsley before she suffered the breakdown and collapse of looking after her invalid aunt she had found it hard to leave the town she and the children had now called home. She could have stayed as Herberts family all pulled together and said they would help any way they could but Dorrie did not want to be a burden, she needed her own family around her and most of all she needed her father. After the false promise of security from her mother and the breakdown Dorrie vowed never to speak or get involved more than she had to with her mother. Poverty was another issue she was faced with, although they now had a roof over their head Dorrie had to work hard to clothe and feed them. Sometimes shoes were not affordable so cardboard was placed in the bottom of their shoes until they could afford a new pair. They had proper meals and nice enough clothes but still had to sacrifice some things. Dorrie worked all the hours she could and still run the house and made sure the children had all her attention and time when she was home. The children had their own fight daily; what with a stigma of having no father a mother that had suffered a breakdown they were taunted at school. David being the eldest had picked up a broad accent and regularly ran out of school because he couldn't be understood. All the same they all worked together and fought against the current. They had to start from scratch and so that's what they did. They all pulled

together to rebuild the life that had been torn apart.
Chapter 6


When Dorrie met Doug, she thought he was handsome and different from all the other men that had tried to court her. He was charming and had grown up in a household full of women. Pauline has gotten quite friendly with his niece and introduced the family to Doug. He had served in the war and since he had returned home was often haunted by the terrible things that he had seen. He used to date girls but nobody had really captured his full attention until he was introduced to Dorrie. Doug was engaged at the time and soon saw to the end of that relationship the moment he grew to know the family round the corner. His sister Ivy put lipstick on his collar one evening so his fiancé soon left him with a trail of words to think about as she slammed the front door. Doug and Ivy laughed and felt relief that he had not entered into something he may later regret.

One night with the assistance of all the women in the house! He decided to bake a stew and take it over to the Shaw household. He had set his sights on her and thought this may be his only chance of getting to know her more. Dorrie opened the door and was dismayed as Doug was standing there with a big pot of food asking if it was acceptable to bring it inside. Dorrie was dumbstruck that a man had cooked for her and let him in. They all ate that night and they talked until the children had gone asleep. Dorrie began to feel herself again and encouraged the time she was spending with Doug. Doug was happy that he had made that stew otherwise he could have ended up marrying someone he wasn't really meant to be with.

After getting to know the family and courting Dorrie in the appropriate manor Doug proposed and Dorrie accepted. They were married with her mothers blessing and Doug moved into Dorries home to take on the role of husband and father.

A few years passed and they were happy, they went on holidays and days away with the children and soon Dorrie learned that she was expecting another child. Dorrie was quite anxious as she was well into her forties by then and she made sure she took it easy and let herself be taken care of for a change. The children were all excited at the new addition to the family and were counting down the days until he or she was here.

Chapter 7

"Take him away, I don't want him" cried Dorrie exhausted from labour and confused about what was going on around her. "I don't know how to care for him" She was getting hysterical now and panicking at all the faces around her and how solemn they were. Doug came into the room and took the baby boy from the midwife. He looked at Dorrie calmly and said " He is coming home

with us and you had better get used to it. You have adapted to harder things than this. He is our son and we will be caring for him." He wasn't abrupt but more matter of fact. He placed the little bundle on Dorries arms and stood there while she looked at the little boys face. Jeffrey was born with Downs something that wasn't detected on any scan because the simply didn't do them. He would need 24 hour attention and would probably always need to live at home. Dorrie was petrified at the thought of not understanding his needs and not being able to care for him in the way he needed.
Doug was confident that they could and they would pull together and make sure that all of their little boys needs were met. The other children were older now and would also help with Jeff and keeping him occupied. After Dorrie took him in her arms she realised what a beautiful baby he was, the shock and panic subsided and she felt overcome with love and adoration.

When they left the hospital Doug instantly became hands on as a father she once again did not receive any support from her mother but was not surprised because as usual she was caught up in her sons' life more than her daughters. As time progressed Jeff did too in leaps and bounds he said odd words and played with the grandchildren in the garden. He loved the paddling pool and the garden so he was happy and content in his environment. Jeff had a mischievous side to him too which often had the whole family in hysterics. He hurled fruit at newcomers and ran around the house without a stitch on in the summer as he couldn't explain he was too hot. Dorrie's mother always made comments about him not buying him presents and cards on birthdays claiming that he wouldn't understand, Dorrie just carried on and let her go about her ways determined she wouldn't let it get to her or drag her down. Doug continued to do odd jobs and chores for her even though she had put her daughter through hell but it showed her in the end that they were better for not rising to her continuous sniping bait. These things are often sent to try us as people, but what doesn't harm us makes us stronger.

Its strange how we deal with situations we are thrust into how we all sometimes wish there was a guidebook we could go back and refer to for the right decision. After all if we bury things for too long they always end up catching up to us in the end.

Dorrie had been facing up to things most of her life knowing it was the only way she had ever gotten through things. She knew Doug wasn't her soul mate but just a companion for the remainder of her journey. He was a haven from what she had previously endured in London. This partnership suited them, it worked so why change it?

Doug's love was the garden. He invested time into it and he was proud of his hard work. Many of the summer days were spent in that garden; dinners, playing, laughing and showing the grandchildren how to plant geraniums. Jeff showed the grandchildren how to empty the freezer in three minutes flat and Dorrie showed them time and love. There was a local park which became an attraction it meant time was spent there and at Dorries. The basketball courts were busy and the bike rides frequent there. Dorrie kept them coming back because she had an aura that everyone wanted to be around and take in. Summer would always be a reminder of those days to her grandchildren; the smell of compost, cut grass and the sound of 60's music playing and floating along to them with the breeze. Its funny how a song can bring back a memory or a particular moment in your life and at that moment make you cry or laugh as you daydream about what once was.

Chapter 8

After all the children had grown up and they had all their own Dorrie was free to concentrate on Jeff fully. Her life was full up of caring and loving him as well as spending time with her family. She visited them. All the summers were packed out with days out and picnics by lakes, swimming, and trips to the seaside. Dorrie had found comfort once again in the life she had rebuilt. She watched her grandchildren grow and go to school. She never mentioned her previous life and her children never questioned her about it. Between everyone they had snippets of memories which were enough to not warrant a cross examination of their mother. Times were

changing and moving on but some ways still lingered in their lives some subjects were still taboo.
Memories from their previous life were not enough to unearth the past.

Dorrie had never been fully aware of what to take to the doctor and what not to. She found a lump and after a few days decided to make an appointment. She was not an alarmist and consulted her family and made sure they kept calm and didn't panic. Whilst she waited to be seen she told herself not to worry and to be brave no matter what the outcome was. "Think of your children, of Jeff and your grandchildren don't let on you're worried Dorrie just be normal and take whatever comes" she told herself. She went into the doctor's room when he called. It was the same surgery she had been going to for years but she had never studied the posters and information around the waiting room so hard before. I suppose everyone that was worried about an appointment knew all the advice sheets of by heart! She sat down and spoke to the doctor then he examined her and told her he would send her for another appointment; this time at the hospital.

Her family rallied round her and her daughter in law went with her to the appointment. They did their tests and told Dorrie she had to wait a few days to hear. Those days were the longest to her children and family that were old enough to comprehend what was hanging over her. After the next doctors appointment Dorrie came home and picked up the phone to her sons and daughters confirming their worst fears. Dorrie had breast cancer.

Dorrie endured chemotherapy and all the side effects, her hair thinned, her appetite was lost and her weight plummeted but she still kept fighting. She seemed to be responding a little as she had all her family around her to be her safety net incase she tumbled. She was trying to lead a normal life and Jeff went into a day centre sometimes just to give Dorrie and Doug a bit of rest bite.

"You know that you are dying" came the words that rang in Dorries ears for the rest of the days that she managed to hold on. The doctor had taken away her dignity and her hope. He had confirmed that she didn't have long left. Doug moved her bed downstairs to make things easier on her. She didn't have far to go to the bathroom and she could relax but still know what was happening. Dorrie saw most of the summer out, she was slowly succumbing to the inevitability of her journey ending. When she opened her eyes a different family member was there holding her frail, soft hand. The sun was shaded by the curtains that remained drawn and the house fell silent.
Everyone crammed time into the last few days and after Dorrie had seen everyone that mattered she finally let go.

We can only imagine and hope that she heard the words uttered in her ear in the final days and that she knew how much she was loved. We can only hope those words and that love echoed in her ear and carried her home.

With her she took the laughter and the tears from within the house, all the reason to go there went right away with her. The house stood encapsulated in time mirroring the emptiness everyone felt in their hearts.

The funeral came and went but closure didn't. Her family got through the service with a blur of tears and the odd smile to old faces coming to pay their respects. Everyone fumbled along into some sort of a routine until a strand of normality returned to their lives.

Time does not make it easier just a little more bearable each day, a little lighter on your heart but never the same. You look for those you loved everywhere, in your dreams, in reality when you are shopping, in the park when you are walking believing that a terrible mistake was made and the woman you watched slip away will return unharmed asking what all the fuss was about. That day never comes.

Instead we are left with a head full of memories and a heart that is heavier some days than others.

With these heavy hearts and minds full of moments, snippets we carry on. We find things to look forward to and reasons we are happy to still be alive and we see that person we once knew emerge farther down the family tree which makes us believe that when our time has come a door will open and there they will be, as they were. Waiting.

Printed in Great Britain
by Amazon